Welcome to the bizarre
PJ Monkman and Sam

We hope you enjoy them

Ann Carlin
& David Wright

Sam meets PJ Monkman

My name is Sam and I'm eleven years old.
I'm quite tall for my age, or so I've been told.
I play lots of sports, I've got lots of friends.
I'm on my computer nearly every weekend.

But not long ago, I met someone new,
I like him a lot and I hope you will too.
May I introduce a good friend of mine?
PJ Monkman, a fellow quite fine.
He has curly red hair and a rather large nose.
His arms and legs are quite thin I suppose.
Well they're certainly long, that is for sure,
as he has to bend down, just to fit through a door!
But the thing I like best is his super wide smile.
It makes you feel happy for quite a long while.

But when he is mad, well you'd better beware.
His eyes turn as red as his curly red hair.
His lips start to curl, so his teeth can be seen,
some of them gold and some of them green!
Not a good look, I'm sure you'll agree.
Keep on his good side, just stick with me.
Then you will find, he is such a good friend,
exciting, funny and really on trend!

Wherever he goes,
you find people will
stare.
I don't think I
explained, just what he
might wear.
Well put it this way, the
colours might clash.
Does red go with
orange, or is it too
brash?
Do silver and gold look
good on a shirt?
Do white and pink
jeans just show the
dirt?
These sorts of things
never bother PJ,
he always continues in
his own special way
Ask too many
questions and he'll just
roll his eyes.
"If I tell you", he says
"there'd be no surprise."
He's a very strange fellow, that's all I can say.
You'd know what I mean if you meet him someday.

Sam and PJ go swimming

The first time I saw him, I was down by a stream.
"Have you caught any fish?" he said with a beam.
I looked in amazement at this man standing there,
his face partially obscured by his curly red hair.
"I wasn't fishing" I said, "I was building a dam,
making a rock pool as deep as I can."

"Oh I love to do that, please can I join in?
My name's PJ Monkman" he said with a grin.
Although he looked strange, I somehow just knew,
he seemed like a man, you could trust through and through.
So he crossed his long legs and sat down next to me.
Then we built up the dam, as happy as can be.
With two people working, we soon formed a deep pool.
When I suddenly noticed something really quite cool.
The area around us had started to change and
the pool looked much larger, it was really quite strange.

"Let's have a swim" PJ cried out with glee.
He stripped down to his trunks, then threw some to me.
"I'm always prepared for a swim in a pool.
You've got to join in for that is the rule!"

So jump in I did and though it was cold,
I thought it was best, to do as I was told!
At the end of our swim, we climbed out and got dressed.
I looked back at the stream and I would never have guessed,
it was just the same size as it had been before!
Would this new friend of mine have more tricks in store.
So my first day with PJ had started quite well.
Would I see him again, it was quite hard to tell.
After our swim in the magical stream,
he just said "Good bye" and vanished it seemed.

I turned my head quickly and looked all around.
But search as I might, he just couldn't be found.
I didn't tell anyone what happened that day.
They'd never believe me, I knew what they'd say.
"I expect you were tired as you played by the stream.
Then you fell fast asleep and had a strange dream."
But I knew it had happened, in my mind not a doubt.
So wherever I went, I kept looking out
for a tall gangly man in bright coloured clothes,
with curly red hair and a rather large nose!

Sam on his mobile

Then a week or so later, I saw him at last.
I was checking my phone just as he walked past.
I caught a glimpse of his shoes, bright purple that day.
"Hi" I called out "are you feeling OK?"
He stopped and he turned and he saw it was me.
"Good to see you again" he said cheerily
"are you ready for another adventure today,
or does that phone leave no time to play?"

I had to laugh, he sounded just like my Mum.
"Of course I've got time, let's go have some fun."

As we wandered along, my phone started to ring.
He said "How much time do you spend on that thing?"

"Quite a lot I suppose, it's not just about chats……"
PJ interrupted "Have you studied the stats?
Think about the e-mails, flying through the sky?
Two billion every second, could just be whizzing by."
It really seemed impossible to take in what he'd said.
I looked around, all sorts of thoughts swirling round my head.

"I mainly use the phone just to play my games
and usually I win, against my best friend James."
PJ then asked "What games do you play?
What keeps you occupied most of the day?"
"Fortnite Battle Royale, I like to get 'skins'.
They give lots of street cred, though they don't help you win.
In the game I fight battles with zombie like creatures,
a big waste of time say most of my teachers!"

Sam enters Fortnite

PJ thought for a while, his brow creased up in a frown.
He stared at my face, then he moved his eyes down.
As his eyes reached my feet, he gave a huge grin.
"I think" he said "that I've found a way in."
"A way into where?" I asked my strange friend.
"It's magic" he said "you will not comprehend."
Well to tell you the truth I was rather annoyed.
Magic is something I've always enjoyed.
PJ thought for a while, his eyes all aflame.
"How would you like to get inside your game?
But once you've been in it, it won't feel the same."
Although I felt scared, I was determined to try.
"Let's do it", I cried "Into battle I'll fly!"
I don't know what he did, but the next thing I knew
I was up in the 'Battle Bus' sat in a queue,
waiting my turn, so I could just glide,
down to the Island without being spied.

I spotted a chance and made a quick leap.
I landed down on the ground in an untidy heap!
But I picked myself up, then I spotted a gun.
I grabbed it and thought "Now its time to have fun!"
I crouched down quite low and sneaked up a hill.
I climbed to the top and what a huge thrill.
The gun was a gold one, it was really quite rare,
the top of its class in this game of warfare.

But what happened next, came as quite a surprise.
When you're playing the game, your character tries,
to shoot someone down and scoop up a prize.
Somehow it felt different, now I really was there,
not sitting at home in my comfy armchair.
So I put down my gun and looked up at the sky.
The next thing I knew, someone said "Hi!"
Of course it was PJ with his super wide smile.
"Welcome back to the world, it's been quite a while!"
"What an adventure I've had" I said to my friend.
"But to tell you the truth, I'm glad it's the end.
I'll still play Fortnite, but I'm pleased it's a game.
In real life I know things would not be the same."
So I said "Goodbye" to Mr PJ.
It really had been a rather strange day.
But I'd still looked forward to the next time we'd meet.
Whatever we did, it would sure be a treat!

Sam and PJ go to the Zoo

But once again PJ vanished from view.
I knew that one day he'd appear out of the blue.
So I didn't really worry, or think something was wrong,
I knew his return would not take too long.
Though in actual fact it was quite a long time,
'till my friend reappeared, my partner in crime!
I wanted an ice cream and as I stood in the queue,
a familiar voice said "Do you fancy the zoo?"
I turned and saw PJ, wearing purple today.
"I'd love to" I said "are you going to pay?"
"No" PJ said "for when we're inside,
we'll work for our keep, let me be your guide."
Should I trust him I wondered, his plan might just fail.
Or it could just work out on a stupendous scale!
"Let's do it!" I cried "The ice cream can wait."
So before very long, we were at the zoo's gate.
As I suspected, PJ had been there before
And soon we were led to the VIP door.

" What's your favourite thing to do at a zoo?"
PJ inquired, though I'd a feeling he knew!
"I like tigers and lions and huge polar bears.
I also like monkeys, but nothing compares
to the brand new aquarium, filled with fishes galore.
Every time I have seen it, I leave wanting more"
PJ walked up to the keeper and had a quick word.
What he said next seemed rather absurd.
"Roll up your sleeves lad, time to get started.
Don't worry you'll like it, so don't be downhearted."
In actual fact, I didn't roll up my sleeves.
Instead I pulled on a wet suit, would you believe!
PJ gave me a snorkel and said "I know you can swim,
so follow me down and our work can begin."
So that's what I did and it's hard to explain,
what fun it was diving again and again.

I cleaned all the rocks at the base of the tank.
Scrubbing them hard, then dropped them down with a clank.
Then back to the surface to collect some fish food.
The big fish pushed the small ones, they were really quite rude!
But I'm sure in the end, they all had a good feed.
No one stayed hungry, they ate all they did need.
As I swam with the fishes, I had quite a surprise,
I saw a friend from my school rubbing his eyes.
His face and his nose were squashed up on the glass.
He was shocked that the swimmer was a boy from his class!

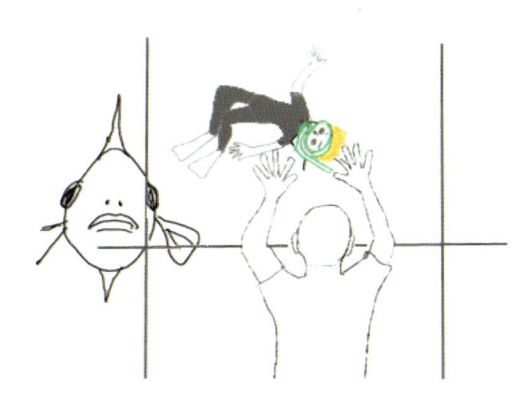

Just at that moment I was feeling quite brave.
So I did my best back flip and gave him a wave!
PJ tapped on my shoulder and signaled to me,
to return to the surface, it was the end of my spree!
So PJ and I climbed out and got dressed.
I told him this trip was one of my best
and the next time he planned to visit the zoo,
to give me a call so I could go too!

Sam and PJ take a balloon ride

For quite a few weeks I worked hard at school.
Exams were in store and I was no fool.
If I did quite well, my parents had said,
I might find a new bike locked up in the shed!
So all thoughts of PJ were put out of my mind.
When my friends asked to play, I politely declined.
My efforts paid off, I came top of my year!
Then before very long, my new bike did appear.
When we broke up for summer, I went out for a ride.
It was a very smart bike and I rode it with pride.
I went past the houses with the greatest of ease,
climbing up hills, then down through the trees.
In the distance I saw an unusual sight.
It was a hot air balloon preparing for flight.
And believe it or not, in the basket below,
PJ Monkman shouted "Hello".

I couldn't believe it, would he really take flight?
But knowing PJ, I knew he just might!
He waved and he said "Do you fancy a ride?"
What should I do, I couldn't decide.
Then a very kind lady standing nearby,
said "I'll guard your bike, give it a try!"

I thought for a minute, but just couldn't refuse.
So I thanked the kind lady and climbed in for my cruise.
As I climbed in the basket, the flames roared out loud
and the balloon floated higher towards a white cloud.
The views were amazing as we continued to rise,
higher and higher into the skies.

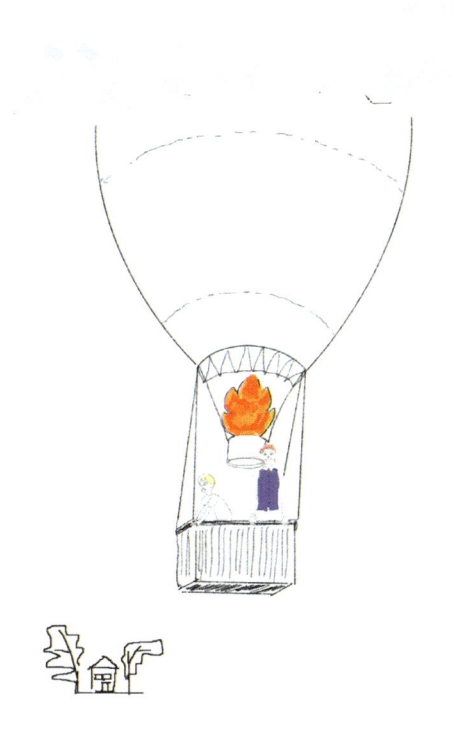

PJ turned down the flames, no sound could be heard.
Neither of us spoke, we did not say a word.
We gazed at the balloon with its colours so bright.
A wonderful moment, a wonderful flight.
Then slowly PJ controlled the balloon down,
landing in a cornfield not far from the town.
We folded the balloon and squashed out the air.
PJ packed it all up with the greatest of care.
So back to the start, it was quite a long hike.
But the kind lady still waited, taking care of my bike.
I thanked her so much and PJ as well,
couldn't wait to get home, my story to tell.

PJ persuades Sam to play his guitar on stage

So the holidays passed in the usual ways,
out with my friends on most of the days.
But I also started to learn something new.
I'd had a guitar for a year, maybe two.
But somehow I never had learned how to play.
So I made a plan, that before my birthday,
I'd aim at least to manage a tune.
I didn't have long as my birthday was soon!

On the bookshelf were manuals, owned by my Dad.
He'd learned to play the guitar when he was a lad.
So we sat down together and he showed me some chords.
He explained if you wanted to reap the rewards,
you should always practice at least once a day.
It would be quite hard, but there was no other way.
So that's what I did and my Dad was quite right.
I practiced and practiced right into the night.
But my hard work paid off and I was really quite proud.
I wondered if I'd ever perform to a crowd?

The very next week, I took my guitar
down to the park, it wasn't too far.
It was sunny and warm, so I sat under a tree,
strumming my tunes, the guitar on my knee.
Then suddenly a shadow obscured my view.
PJ smiled as he said "I thought it was you!"
I was eager to show him how well I could play.
As I strummed my guitar, PJ started to sway.
I laughed and I said "Shall I sing my new song?
It's really quite short, so it won't take too long."
"Yes" PJ said "show me what you can do.
Can't wait to hear it, I love something new"

So I took a deep breath and started to sing.
I was nervous at first, then got into the swing.
The tune was quite catchy, with a foot tapping beat.
Before very long, PJ was up on his feet.
His curly red hair blew around in the wind.
"You're a budding pop star," he cried as he grinned
"I've got an idea, so just follow me.
I know a place you can sing, that's not under a tree!"
It's hard to say 'no' to PJ in full swing.
So I grabbed my guitar and did not say a thing.

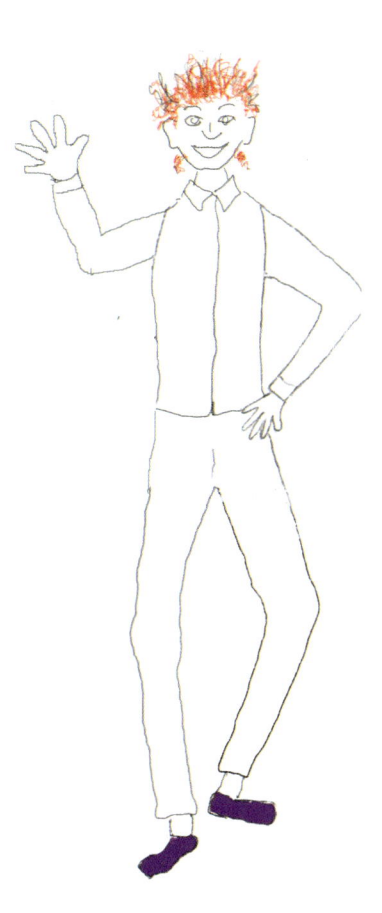

I followed my friend to the edge of the park,
passing tall trees, it was really quite dark.
But then in the distance I saw a huge stage.
It was covered with lights and looked really 'space age'
Quite a few people were sitting around
on bright coloured blankets spread on the ground.
Then onto the stage came someone I knew.
PJ appeared from out of the blue!
He gave a big wave, then pointed to me.
Up you come Sam" he said with great glee.

I gasped with amazement and shook my head hard.
I just couldn't do it, he'd caught me off guard.
But as I've said before, PJ won't let you say 'no'
and I found myself walking to be in the show!
As I climbed on the stage, the crowd started to cheer.
There was no turning back now, that was quite clear.
So I tuned my guitar and started to play.
As I sang my new song, PJ cried out "Hurray!"

As I got to the chorus, the crowd all joined in
and all I could see was PJ's huge grin.
At the end of the song, I stepped down from the stage.
What an achievement for a boy of my age!

PJ and I walked home through the park.
I had to get home before it got dark.
But when we had nearly got to my door,
I turned to PJ, but he'd gone, as before.
I smiled to myself and I knew it was true,
There's no limit at all, in what you can do.
So always remember, though you don't know PJ,
if you keep looking out, you could meet him someday!

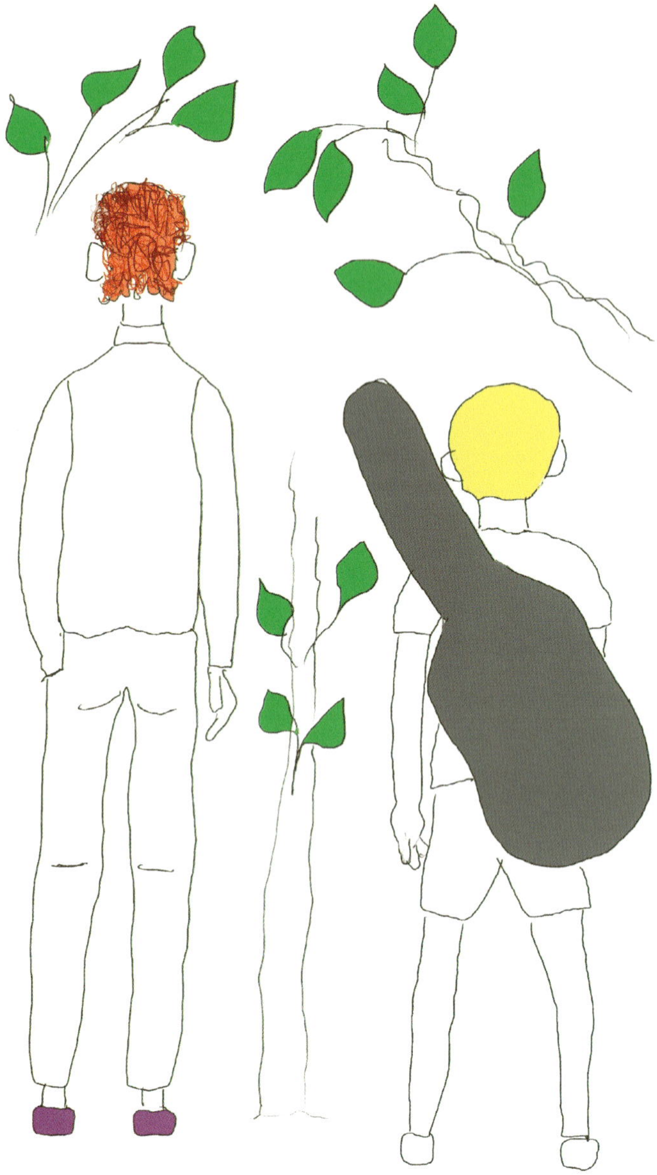

Also available by the same author:

Sliding down rainbows

Book 1 The adventure begins
story by Ann Carlin
pictures by David Wright

Edward and Eleanor discover a magic rainbow in the corner of their room and go sliding down it to a magical kingdom

Sliding down rainbows

Book 2 The fairground
story by Ann Carlin
pictures by David Wright

Edward and Eleanor go sliding down a magic rainbow to a funfair run by dogs

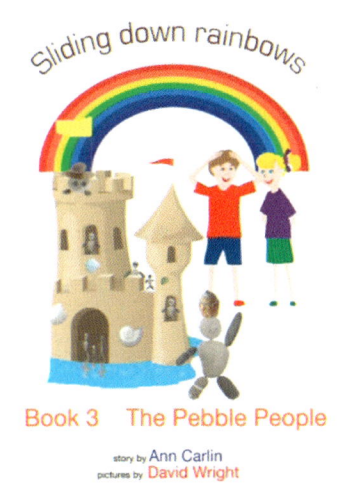

Sliding down rainbows

Book 3   The Pebble People

story by Ann Carlin
pictures by David Wright

Edward and Eleanor
go sliding down a magic
raiunbow to a beach
full of pebble people

**Dexter James,
the super cool DJ**

story by Ann Carlin
pictures by David Wright

Dexter is a young boy who
dreams of being a DJ.
He is given the chance to
mix and scratch some music
at a secret music venue.

Zac and the Cloud

Zachary hitches a ride on a talking cloud and gets to see his house from above.

story by Ann Carlin
pictures by David Wright

Zac becomes a Champion

Zac meets his magical friend Clive the cloud and goes on another adventure.
Zac enters a computer game and Clive helps him achieve a record score.

story by Ann Carlin
pictures by David Wright

Mikey and the Bee

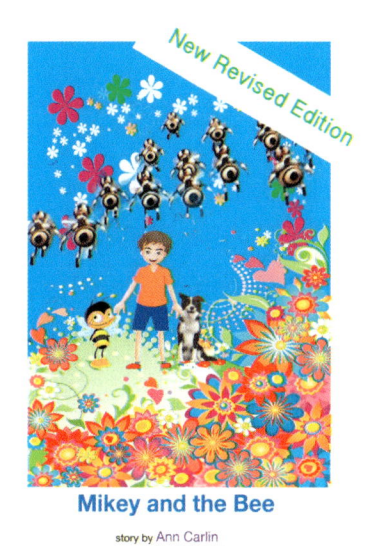

story by Ann Carlin
pictures by David Wright

Mikey and his dog Alfie help a lazy bee to collect nectar to turn into honey.

Mikey and his dog Alfie meet a story telling ladybird.

Mikey and the Ladybird

story by Ann Carlin
pictures by David Wright

Mikey and the Frog

story by Ann Carlin
pictures by David Wright

Mikey and his dog Alfie stumble across some frogs who are holding a sports day and end up helping them with the events.

This is a story of a group of children all who possess magical powers and go on fantasy adventures where they use them

The Magic Shed Club

Printed in Poland
by Amazon Fulfillment
Poland Sp. z o.o., Wrocław